WHY THIS IS AN EASY READER

- This story has been carefully written so that it will keep the young reader's interest high.

- It is told in a simple, open style with a strong rhythm that adds enjoyment both to reading aloud and silent reading.

- Only 168 different words have been used, with plurals and root words counted once.

- There is a very high percentage of words repeated. *It is this skillful repetition which helps the child to read independently.* Seeing words again and again, he "practices" the vocabulary he knows, and actually learns the words that are new.

ABOUT THE WORDS IN THIS STORY

- 76 words — *more than one-third the total vocabulary* — have been used at least three times.

- 49 words have been used at least five times.

- Some words have been used 34 times.

CHOOSE FROM THESE EASY READERS

Mr. Pine's Mixed-up Signs

Story and Pictures by
LEONARD KESSLER

Editorial Consultant
LILIAN MOORE

WONDER BOOKS

1107 Broadway, New York 10, N. Y.

Introduction

These books are meant to help the young reader discover what a delightful experience reading can be. The stories are such fun that they urge the child to try his new reading skills. They are so easy to read that they will encourage and strengthen him as a reader.

The adult will notice that the sentences aren't too long, the words aren't too hard, and the skillful repetition is like a helping hand. What the child will feel is: "This is a good story—and I can read it myself!"

For some children, the best way to meet these stories may be to hear them read aloud at first. Others, who are better prepared to read on their own, may need a little help in the beginning—help that is best given freely. Youngsters who have more experience in reading alone—whether in first or second or third grade—will have the immediate joy of reading "all by myself."

These books have been planned to help all young readers grow—in their pleasure in books and in their power to read them.

Lilian Moore
Specialist in Reading
Formerly of Division of Instructional Research,
New York City Board of Education

Mr. Pine made signs.

He made signs that said

He made signs that said

He made signs that said

And signs that said

7

Mr. Pine made all the signs

in Little Town.

A town needs many signs.

It needs signs for roads. . .

and streets

and stores.

Mr. Pine made them all

for Little Town.

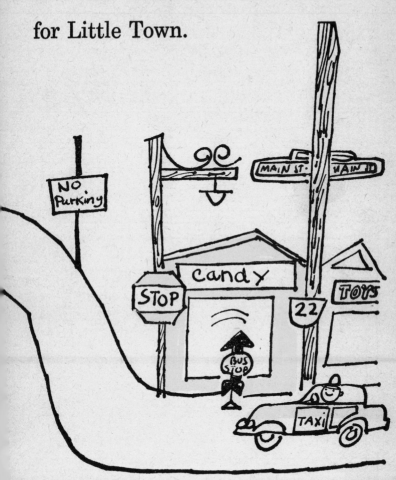

He painted big signs.

He painted little signs.

He painted signs with words.

He painted signs with pictures.

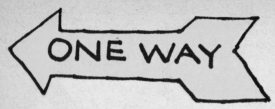

"Go this way."

"Go that way."

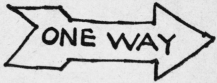

Or signs that said:

"Look out—a road will cross."

"Slow Down! Hole in the road!"

Yes, Little Town
had all the signs
a town could need.

13

But, little by little, the signs
in Little Town
got old.
The rain and the snow
fell on the signs.

The wind blew them
and the hot sun baked them.

Soon no one
could tell
what the signs said.

"We need new signs,"
said the Mayor of Little Town.
"I will go to see Mr. Pine."
And he did.

"Mr. Pine, we need new signs
all
over
Little
Town,"
said the Mayor.
"Will you make them for us?"

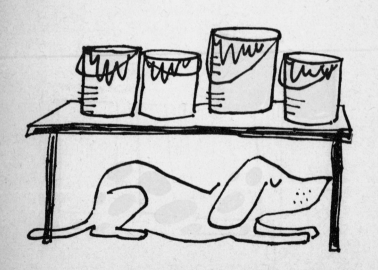

"Oh, yes, yes," said Mr. Pine.

"I like to make signs.

I will paint them all

and I will put them up, too."

"We need them
right away," said the Mayor.
"I will do them
right away," said Mr. Pine.
"You will have them all
in one week!"

The next week Mr. Pine

painted and painted

and painted.

He painted big signs.

He painted little signs.

He painted round signs.

He painted red signs

and blue signs and green signs.

At the end of the week

all the new signs were done.

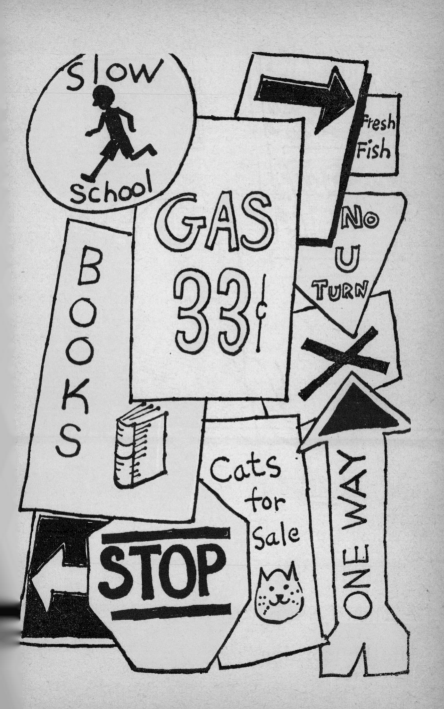

"Now I must let the signs dry,"
said Mr. Pine.

"Then I can put them up
in the morning."

In the morning Mr. Pine

got out of bed.

"Where are my glasses?"

Mr. Pine said.

25

He looked here:

and here:

and here:

and even HERE!

He looked everywhere.
But he did not see
his glasses.
"Where can they be?"
he said.
"Oh, dear, everything
looks so funny!
I wish I had my glasses."

Everything did look
funny.
But Mr. Pine had
to put up the signs.
So out he went.

Soon the new signs were up

all over Little Town.

Mr. Pine did not know it,

but the signs looked funny, too!

The town looked like this:

and like this:

and like THIS!

Did you ever see a town look
like this?

Mr. Jones, the baker, went

to open his store.

The sign over the door

of his store said

"HATS FOR SALE"

Mr. Clark went to open

his shoe store.

The sign on the window

said "GAS 33¢"

Mr. Hill went to open
his candy store.
The sign
on the door
said
"PET SHOP
Cats and Dogs
for Sale."

Mr. Brown went
to open his bookstore.
What did he see?
A big sign
that said
"NO PARKING
AT ANY TIME"

Every sign on every store

on every street

on every road

was new,

but

they were

all

MIXED UP.

Over the bank

the sign said

"BREAD"

The sign on Main Street

said

"Candy 5¢"

And the sign

on the Mayor's door

said

"THIS WAY

TO THE

ZOO"

"Find Mr. Pine!"

cried the Mayor.

"Find him fast!"

Soon everyone was looking

for Mr. Pine.

Where was Mr. Pine?

He was looking

for his glasses.

"Where can they be?" he said

again and again.

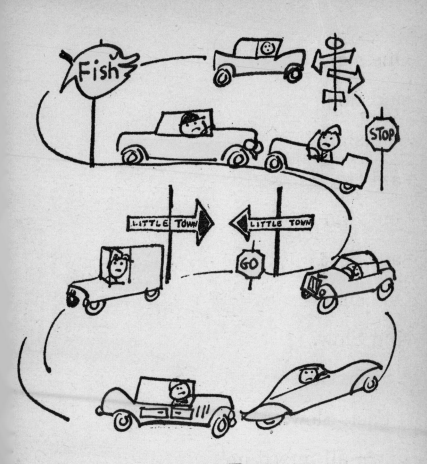

The cars in Little Town

were going round

and round.

Everyone was

all mixed up.

One sign
said Stop.
One sign
said Go.
One sign
said Fast.
One sign
said Slow.
Stop. Go.
Fast. Slow.
—all mixed up!

"Find Mr. Pine!"

cried the Policeman.

And where was Mr. Pine?

Mr. Pine was still looking

for his glasses.

"Did I put them here?

Or did I put them here?" he said.

"I must find
my glasses. I want
to see all my fine
new signs."

He looked everywhere.

At last he looked here:

And there they were!

How happy Mr. Pine was

to have found

his glasses!

He ran to the window

and looked out.

"Oh, no!" he said.

"Oh, no!"

He saw this:

"Oh! Oh!" cried Mr. Pine.

"What a mix-up!"

He ran to find

the Mayor.

The Mayor

was running

to find him.

"Mr. Pine," said the Mayor.

"Mr. Mayor,"

said Mr. Pine.

Then together they cried,

"The signs are

all mixed up!"

"I will fix them
right away,"
said Mr. Pine.
And he did.

Soon the new signs

were in the right

place.

Soon Little Town looked

all right again.

But no one will ever forget

Mr. Pine and the mixed-up day!